THREE GIFTS FROM THE GREEN DRAGON

and other stories from Chinese literature

Catherine Lim
illustrator Chen Tian-Ci

the
W

A Target Book
Published in 1985
by the Paperback Division of
W. H. Allen & Co. PLC
44 Hill Street, London W1X 8LB

Printed in Great Britain by
Cox & Wyman Ltd, Reading

ISBN 0 426 20196 5

Contents

HOW JUDGE NGAI GOT RID OF THE FOUR SNAKES

In the district of Lung Yau in the Shansi Province of China, there was a very rich and greedy landowner called Lam Ngok Pa. This landowner had grown very rich and powerful as a result of cheating the people and forcing them to do what he wanted. For instance, if he wanted a piece of land belonging to someone else, he offered a low price for it. The owner had no choice but to accept Lam Ngok Pa's offer, knowing that otherwise he would be severely beaten up by Lam's men, a band of merciless ruffians.

Now, Lam was able to do all this because he was the close friend of the Prince and the Prime Minister, two equally wicked men. These three men with their evil ways became known as "the three snakes". Protected in this way, Lam went on cheating the people and growing richer and more powerful.

The governor of the district looked on helplessly. He was a good and upright man, but he knew that as long as the wicked landowner had the friendship of the Prince and the Prime Minister, there was nothing he could do. His last hope lay in Judge Ngai Sheung Cheng.

Now Judge Ngai was the bravest judge anyone had ever known. He showed no fear of anyone, no matter how powerful that person might be. All he was concerned about was to be fair and to bring peace and happiness to the people.

The governor sent for Judge Ngai to be the magistrate of his district. All the people were full of joy when the Judge came, for they believed that this wise and brave judge would at last save them from the evil Lam.

Alas! Their hopes were dashed. When the people presented a petition against Lam to the Judge, pointing out all his evil deeds, Judge Ngai tore up the petition and said angrily to them, "How dare you tell me such lies about Lam Ngok Pa? He is a good man, much respected by the Prince and the Prime Minister. How can you call him a thief and a murderer? Now get out, all of you!"

The people shook their heads in disbelief and sorrow. So even Judge Ngai feared Lam Ngok Pa. The three "snakes" were going to be stronger than ever. What greater miseries they were going to suffer!

All this was reported to Lam by his men. The landowner was delighted. He was pleased to know that even Judge Ngai was afraid of him and wanted to be a friend.

Soon after this, Judge Ngai came to visit him with a handsome present. Lam found, to his delight, that the Judge was most anxious to be his friend. That suited him fine. He often invited the Judge to dinner in his big, beautiful mansion. Meanwhile, he went on cheating the people and making their lives more miserable than ever. Of course, the landowner did not know that all this was part of the clever Judge's plan to destroy him and his evil friends. The three "snakes" had to be got rid of.

One day, after dinner, Lam was in a talkative mood and began to boast of his crimes to Judge Ngai.

"I have no need to fear anything because the Prince is my good friend," he boasted. "See this gold ring? It has the Prince's own signature on it. The Prince wears a ring exactly like this. There are only two rings of this kind in the world. Whenever the Prince sends me a secret message, he sends along his ring, so that I know the messenger is truly from him."

Judge Ngai nodded. He was carefully storing up all

this information for future use.

One night soon after this, he went to Lam and said to him in a serious voice, "The Prime Minister is dead. There is a new Prime Minister at the Palace who doesn't like you since you and the Prince are such close friends. I hear that this new Prime Minister will set the Emperor against you. I fear for you, my friend!"

Lam became very nervous. The thought of losing his power frightened him.

The next night, a messenger arrived at his mansion carrying the same message from the Prince. The messenger carried the Prince's gold ring. Lam was most alarmed. What he did not know was that the messenger was Judge Ngai's own man and that the gold ring had been secretly made by a goldsmith friend of his.

Lam began to wring his hands in distress. "Oh, what shall I do?" he cried to Judge Ngai.

"I'll tell you what you can do," said the Judge. "Write down all the crimes you have committed, giving details about them, in a letter to the Prince. This is to enable the Prince to study them carefully so that he can defend you before the Emperor. The Prince is a clever man, you know. I shall take this letter myself to the Prince as we may not be able to trust the servants with such an important document."

Lam was most pleased with the plan. He wrote down in detail all the crimes as the Judge had advised. There were so many crimes that by the time he had finished the pages made up a fairly large parcel! He quickly slipped out of his house with the thick letter and hurried to Judge Ngai's house.

Breathlessly, he handed the letter to the Judge.

"Here it is," he said. "I've written down every single one of my crimes in my letter."

"It's a very long letter, isn't it?" said the Judge softly.

Then, to Lam's amazement, he gave a signal. As if from nowhere, a group of officers and guards appeared and surrounded Lam. They led him to a large courtroom where many people were waiting. They were those whom Lam had cheated or harmed in one

way or another. One by one, they stood up to accuse him of various misdeeds. After he had heard their accusations, Judge Ngai sentenced the evil landlord to death. How the people rejoiced!

One "snake" had been got rid of. Now the other two had to be dealt with. Ngai made a copy of the letter which Lam had written. He then disguised himself as one of Lam's messengers. With the Prince's ring, which he had taken from the evil landlord, he journeyed to the royal city.

There, he went straight to see the Prince. As the Judge was able to produce the ring, the Prince did not suspect anything.

He read Lam's long letter. Then he laughed out loud. "The silly fool! Imagine being frightened of such things! I will write and tell him not to be such a coward. The old Prime Minister is still alive and together we will protect all our friends!" He wrote this down in a letter, all the while chuckling over Lam's cowardice.

Judge Ngai eagerly took the Prince's letter and, still dressed as the messenger, secretly went to see the Emperor himself. He told the Emperor of how the Prince and the Prime Minister had been protecting the evil landowner Lam and others like him.

The Emperor, a just man, was very angry when he heard all this. He ordered the Prince and the Prime Minister to be brought before the Chief Judge of the Palace. The Chief Judge would pass sentence on them.

Now this Chief Judge was just as corrupt as the three "snakes". That made four "snakes". Knowing he could not be trusted, Judge Ngai began to think very hard. How could he get rid of all four "snakes"?

Before the trial, the Chief Judge asked to see the two letters written by Lam and the Prince. Judge Ngai handed them over. The letters were strong proof of the guilt of the landowner, the Prince and the Prime Minister, but the Chief Judge was eager to protect his friends. He had the letters secretly destroyed.

At the trial before the Emperor, he told all those gathered there that the letters had been accidentally destroyed in a fire. There was therefore no proof of the guilt of the two men and he would have to put an end to the matter. There were smiles of relief on the faces of the Prime Minister and the Prince.

At this point, Judge Ngai took something out of his pocket. It was the two letters which Lam and the Prince had written. Those which he had given to the Chief Judge had been only copies! When the Chief Judge heard this he turned pale. He stared with his mouth wide open like a goldfish. Everyone was looking at him.

Judge Ngai said as he handed the letters to the Emperor, "I knew that the Chief Judge would destroy the letters so I gave him only copies of them, and kept the real ones."

The Emperor read the letters. He looked severely at the Chief Judge, the Prime Minister and the Prince.

"You are three evil men," he said. "To think that I have been surrounded by people who cheat and lie and bring misery to others while pretending to do their duty! This cannot go on. A country can never enjoy peace and prosperity with snakes like yourselves. Fortunately, we have men like Judge Ngai who is brave enough to expose you to the world!"

The three evil men were duly punished and disgraced. Judge Ngai was made Prime Minister. With his wisdom and courage, he guided the country to prosperity and happiness. People loved to tell the story of how this brave man got rid of not one, but four "snakes"!

ONE COPPER COIN

YUE GUANG AND YUE GUO were two poor brothers who lived in a small village in China a very long time ago. They were both very young when their parents died, Yue Guang being only six and Yue Guo five. An uncle took care of them, but after some time, he too died, leaving the two boys alone in the world.

Yue Guang and Yue Guo were therefore homeless and wandered about the village, living on whatever food was offered them by kind villagers. Often they went hungry.

While Yue Guo, the younger brother, was bright and alert and ready to do whatever he could to earn his daily meals, Yue Guang was inclined to be rather lazy. Yue Guo did not mind carrying heavy bundles of wood or drawing buckets of water from the well or feeding the pigs for the villagers in order to earn a bowl of rice. Yue Guang, however, preferred to lie in the shade of a tree nibbling a blade of grass and idling his time away. Fortunately, Yue Guo usually managed to earn enough food for both of them.

Although they were different in character, both

brothers cherished a common dream. When they were little boys, their parents and uncle had told them stories of the Great Prince who lived in another part of the land, far away.

The Great Prince was famous throughout the breadth and length of China as a magnificent warrior, a splendid horseman, a courageous hunter and the wisest man who ever lived. Indeed, there were so many admirable abilities and qualities of the Great Prince, that it was impossible to describe them all. It was said, moreover, that his appearance was remarkable. He was tall and strong, with a face that shone like the sun, and with the dark, piercing eyes of a god. He was described as the wisest man on earth, who could see through all skilful and cunning deceptions. Nobody could ever trick him.

Many indeed were the stories told about the grandeur, magnificence and wisdom of the Great Prince. Yue Guang and Yue Guo used to listen open-mouthed when their parents and uncle related these stories. It was said that he was seldom seen, and that many people who hoped to catch a glimpse of him went away disappointed.

The boys' admiration for the Great Prince continued to grow. It became the overpowering dream of Yue Guang and Yue Guo to see the Great Prince and serve him. They longed to belong to his troop of horsemen which was said to be the finest in the world.

One day, when they were seventeen and sixteen years old respectively, Yue Guang and Yue Guo decided to go to the region where the Great Prince lived. They set off, filled with eager ambition. They were still very poor, having lived all these years by doing odd jobs for the people in the village.

Yue Guang had not left behind his lazy habits. He still liked to rest comfortably in the shade of trees while his brother did the hard work. He would only do work which suited him or which was not too taxing on his strength. He would never take on a lowly job such as cleaning a pig's sty or gathering dung as manure for the vegetable plots.

Yue Guo, on the other hand, cheerfully did everything that came his way, whether the task was lowly or not. He was always bright and alert and looking out for opportunities to improve himself.

The two brothers finally arrived in the domain of the Great Prince, but alas! They could not get a glimpse of him. Day in, day out, they loitered near the Great Prince's palace, a huge, splendid structure on a hill — but he never came out. Perhaps he was fighting a war in another part of the land; perhaps he was secretly moving among his people, observing them as they went about their work. Nobody knew anything. When Yue Guang and Yue Guo asked those living around if they knew anything about the whereabouts of the Great Prince, they only received blank stares. The Great Prince was indeed living up to his reputation as a very mysterious person.

"We cannot afford to wait idly doing nothing," said Yue Guo. "We must find work soon, or we'll starve."

There appeared few jobs to do in this new region that they had come to. Yue Guang was content with things as they were, leaving his younger brother, as usual, to think out ways of earning money for food.

One day, as Yue Guang and Yue Guo were wandering near the Great Prince's palace, wondering if they would ever see him, they noticed a man feeding a horse. He was probably one of the Prince's grooms.

The brothers watched as he fed some hay to the horse and then cleaned its coat. He looked at them and asked if they would be interested in getting a job. Yue Guo's eyes lit up.

"What sort of job?" asked Yue Guang.

"Well," said the groom with a cunning gleam in his eye, "I hate to clean my stable, for the smell of dung makes me feel quite sick! If you will do it for me, I shall give you a copper coin at the end of the week!"

The faces of the brothers fell. They had not expected such a lowly job, at such a mean pay.

"What, a copper coin for a week of hard work! And filthy work at that!" cried Yue Guang impatiently. "No, thank you! You will not find me such a fool as to accept it."

Yue Guo, however, was thinking over the matter carefully. He was inclined to take on the job, unattractive though it seemed. After all, a copper coin was better than nothing, and besides, he was getting restless with nothing to do. If he worked hard enough, the groom might decide to give him more money in future.

"I'll take it," said Yue Guo, stepping forward. "I shall begin right away, if you wish."

"What! You're a fool, Yue Guo!" cried Yue Guang angrily. "A copper coin! What can you do with a copper coin?" So saying, he strode away in disgust.

Yue Guo began his new work. He was a very industrious worker. He cleaned the stable thoroughly even though the smell of dung was most unpleasant.

At the end of the week, the groom gave him one copper coin. Yue Guo looked at it thoughtfully. It was a very, very small amount of money, so small he doubted whether he could buy anything with it.

Holding the coin carefully in his hand, Yue Guo took a walk. It led him to a busy marketplace. Yue Guo's mouth watered at the sight of the steaming hot food sold at the stalls, but knew his copper coin could buy him nothing.

He stood in front of a stall at which seeds of all kinds were sold in little sacks. There was an old woman sitting behind the rows of seeds, looking curiously at him.

"I think these are lettuce seeds. How healthy they look," remarked Yue Guo, looking at the sack in front of him.

"Would you like to buy some?" asked the old woman.

"Yes. How many lettuce seeds can I buy with one copper coin?" asked Yue Guo.

"One copper coin! Why, you can't even buy two lettuce seeds with that!" laughed the old woman. She found Yue Guo a rather strange but amusing young man.

"If I put this copper coin into the sack of lettuce seeds and pull it up again, I bet it will have more than two seeds on it," remarked Yue Guo.

"You can try," said the woman. "For your copper coin, I will let you have all the seeds that stick to it!"

Quick as lightning, without the old woman noticing it, Yue Guo put the coin into his mouth so that it was wet with his saliva and then dipped it into the little sack of lettuce seeds. He brought it up again with many of the seeds clinging closely to it! The old woman was astonished but she only laughed and good-naturedly kept her promise.

Yue Guo returned with the small cluster of lettuce seeds. He took them to a plot of ground near the palace that nobody seemed to want. Very carefully, he planted the seeds into the earth and watered them. Then he went to the groom and told him he would continue to clean his horse's stable, even if he were not paid any money! All he wanted was the horse's dung.

"The horse's dung! Why, you can have all of it!" laughed the groom.

When Yue Guang saw his brother carrying the dung, he too laughed. Yue Guo took the dung away and used it as manure for his growing lettuce. With Yue Guo's care, and the nourishment they derived from the dung, the lettuce plants thrived. Very soon,

big luscious lettuces appeared, ready to be eaten!

Yue Guo harvested them, and prepared to sell them in the market. As he looked at the lettuces, so big and juicy, he thought to himself, "What a pity I cannot offer these to the Great Prince. How I wish I could see him now and let him have these beautiful lettuces! But he's too great to care for such things as these lettuces of mine!"

"No, he's not," said someone.

Yue Guo turned around and saw before him a

person so tall and handsome and bright that he could hardly believe his eyes. The Great Prince! What a resplendent, magnificent figure! Yue Guo could only stare, speechless.

"I know about you and your copper coin," said the Great One softly. "I was pleased to see you did not despise the work of cleaning the horse's stable or the copper coin you were offered. From such humble beginnings, great things can come!"

To his delight, Yue Guo was taken by the Great Prince into his palace and made one of the palace serving men. He worked so hard that he was very rapidly promoted. From one job he ascended to another until by the time he was twenty, he had become the Great Prince's closest adviser. He was so much trusted by the Prince that he was soon given command of a large region.

He prospered till the end of his days, and when, in his old age, people asked him to tell the story of his life, he would always say, "Well, I'll begin with the copper coin . . . "

A TIGER'S REMORSE

THE OLD WIDOW Pao was filled with grief. Tears coursed down her thin, furrowed cheeks, and sobs shook her small, thin body. Her only son had just been killed by a tiger.

He had gone up to the hills near his home to cut some firewood for his old mother. A large, ferocious tiger roaming the hills had pounced on him and killed him. Somebody had seen the tragedy happen and rushed home to tell the widow Pao. Her grief was so great that all her neighbours wept with her.

"Oh wicked, wicked tiger, to kill my only son, my beloved son!" mourned the old woman.

"The wicked beast should be arrested for the murderer it is, and put to death!" cried one of the neighbours.

Old widow Pao suddenly stopped crying. There was a look of grim determination on her face. "Yes, that's what I'll do," she said. "I'll go to the magistrate and tell him to arrest the tiger!"

So widow Pao went before the magistrate of the district, knelt down and told him the whole story. Then she begged him to arrest the evil tiger. The magistrate was astonished by her request. He wanted to laugh out loud at the thought of arresting a tiger and bringing it to court, but the old woman was looking at him so earnestly, that he had to look serious.

He explained to her, with great patience, that this was not a thing that could be done. However, she would not listen to him, but kept insisting that he issue a warrant of arrest against the tiger that had killed her only son.

The magistrate would have got impatient with a younger person, but he felt sorry for the old white-haired widow. He was at a loss as to what to do. Finally, he turned to his attendants to ask if any of them could find a way out of the tricky situation.

One of the attendants, a young man called Xiao Hua, happened to have drunk a little too much rice wine. He was in a cheerful mood and he stepped forward eagerly and said, "Leave everything to me! I shall arrest the wicked beast and bring it to court!"

So the magistrate issued the warrant and the old widow Pao went back home.

When the effect of the rice wine had worn off, Xiao Hua suddenly realised, with fright, his rash promise. He felt very foolish. How could he possibly arrest a tiger? He decided to go to the magistrate, confess that he had been a fool and ask to be let off such an impossible task.

"No, no, young man!" cried the magistrate. "You said you could arrest the tiger, and arrest it you will! I shall give you a week to do this, no more!"

Xiao Hua was most alarmed. He knew the magistrate would not listen to any plea for mercy. With a sad heart, he went home and wondered how he could accomplish his task. Arrest a tiger! How stupid he had been to boast he could do that! Xiao Hua cursed the rice wine that had brought him all this trouble.

Five days passed. Xiao Hua was at his wits' end. What was he to do? If he did not bring in the tiger, the magistrate was sure to give him several hundred blows with the bamboo.

On the sixth day, in his desperation, Xiao Hua hurried to a temple outside the town to pray. He fell on his knees and prayed for help. He promised that if his prayers were answered, he would never get drunk again.

Suddenly, to his astonishment and fear, he saw a huge, ferocious-looking tiger come into the temple. It walked slowly towards him. Xiao Hua was about to shriek in his terror, when he saw the tiger sitting down beside him. What was more amazing was that the tiger dropped its head, as if it were ashamed of something, and two large tears rolled down from its eyes!

Xiao Hua's fear was gone. He said to the tiger, "O tiger, are you the beast which killed the old widow Pao's son?"

The tiger nodded its head.

"O tiger," continued Xiao Hua, "you have committed a murder and I must arrest you and bring you to court. Allow me to bind you with this rope!"

So saying, he drew a coil of rope from his pocket and threw it over the animal's neck. The tiger meekly allowed the rope to be put round its neck. Its head still drooped, and its eyes were still filled with tears.

Xiao Hua led the tiger before the magistrate. Imagine the amazement of the magistrate and all his attendants!

"Tiger, did you kill widow Pao's son?" asked the magistrate sternly, quickly getting over his astonishment.

The tiger nodded its head sorrowfully.

"Well, tiger," said the magistrate. "It is the law that murderers must be put to death. Your crime was especially great because your victim was the old widow's only son. Now she has no one to look after her in her old age!"

The tiger continued to look sorrowful. It turned its head in the direction of the old widow, and two large tears again formed in its eyes and dropped to the ground.

"Tiger, I'm sorry to have to pronounce this sentence, but you must be taken out and put to death now!" exclaimed the magistrate. "Only in this way will the old widow Pao be satisfied."

"Wait!" cried the old woman. "Don't put the tiger to death! I can see that it is filled with remorse. Let the tiger take the place of my dead son, and I shall be satisfied!"

All were surprised at the old woman's words, but she was most serious.

"All right," said the magistrate, who was quite relieved, for he did not wish to put the tiger to death.

Turning to the tiger, he said solemnly, "Tiger, listen very carefully. To pay for your crime, you must now take the place of old widow Pao's son. You must take good care of the old woman just as her son would have done if he were alive."

The tiger nodded assent. Now it was no longer shedding tears.

So, the old widow Pao took the tiger home with her. What a good son the tiger proved to be! It did everything to make the old woman's life comfortable. Every morning when she opened the door of her cottage, she would find something of value there.

Once, there was a dead deer. It was a large handsome animal. The old woman kept some of the flesh for her own food and sold the rest together with the deer skin and horns which were used in the making of certain medicines. She got a fairly large sum of money for all these. On another occasion, the tiger laid a large stack of firewood at her doorstep. She was never without firewood after that.

On yet another occasion she found some roots which the tiger had obviously unearthed from the forest.

"Why!" exclaimed the widow Pao in delight. "These are ginseng roots which I can make into brews to cure the aches in my body!"

She had so many of these valuable roots that she could even afford to give some to her friends. The widow Pao was never healthier or happier. She was never without food or money.

Most important of all, the tiger became her close companion. It would sit quietly beside her and allow itself to be stroked affectionately. At night it guarded her house, so that she never needed to fear burglars or robbers.

The widow lived to a ripe old age and the tiger took care of her till the end of her days. When she died, the tiger wept so sorrowfully that the neighbours wept with it. It sat by her grave weeping, and refused to be coaxed away. Finally it died in its sorrow and was buried beside the old widow.

Everybody said that the tiger was the best "son" any mother could have. For many years after that the people often told the story of the tiger who had felt so much remorse for its crime that it spent the rest of its life paying for it.

SHADE FOR SALE

THERE HAD NEVER been anyone as greedy as Xiao-Bo, everybody in the village agreed. Xiao-Bo was the richest man in the village — and the stingiest.

He thought only of making money from the people around him. He owned several acres of land dotted with prosperous farms, had many cowhands and made a lot of money selling the fowls and pigs from his farm and the fruit and vegetables from his large, well-tended gardens. However, he paid his workers very low wages. He had no pity whatever on the poor people, and went about in his silk gown and silk cap thinking of ways of getting more money.

One morning, he sat in his house looking out through the window into the garden. He looked with pleasure upon the large pear tree that grew close to the wall around his garden. It was laden with fruit. Soon Xiao-Bo would have all the lovely pears plucked, taken to the markets in the city and sold at a good profit.

Suddenly, he noticed a large, ripe pear dropping from a branch hanging over the garden wall. He rushed out to see a little boy picking up the fruit and putting it to his mouth.

"Hey, give it back, that's my pear!" cried Xiao-Bo angrily.

"But I found it outside your garden. I didn't steal it!" cried the little boy, looking quite frightened.

"It's my property, give it back!" said Xiao-Bo sternly. Then he noticed that the boy had already bitten into the pear.

"You've spoilt my pear, you must pay for it now!" cried Xiao-Bo.

"I've no money!" said the little boy.

Xiao-Bo searched the boy's pockets and found a coin. "I'll take that, it's payment for my pear," he said, dropping the coin into the pocket of his silk robe.

"But it's the money my mother gave me to buy some sauce for her rice!" cried the little boy with tears in his eyes.

"You should have thought of that before taking what belongs to others! Be off with you now!" said Xiao-Bo and he walked back to his house.

On another day, Xiao-Bo was walking along the road leading to the village market. He saw a cart carrying a load of vegetables being drawn by two bullocks. He recognised with pleasure that the cart and bullocks belonged to him. He owned many such carts and bullocks.

Suddenly he noticed one of the bullocks easing itself and dropping a huge pile of dung on the ground. A man near by ran up and scooped the hot, moist dung on to a brick tile. He was going to use the dung to fertilise his vegetable garden as he couldn't afford to buy fertilisers.

"Hey, you, what are you doing? That's my property! It came from my bullock!" roared Xiao-Bo, rushing forward.

"But it dropped on the ground! I didn't steal it from your house," said the man.

"You must pay for it," said Xiao-Bo sternly.

"B . . . b . . . but I have no money," stammered the poor man.

It was true. Xiao-Bo searched him thoroughly and found not a single small coin on him. "All right, you'll have to pay for the dung with some vegetables from your garden," said Xiao-Bo, looking very fierce. "It's the law. You cannot take what belongs to another without paying for it. I always abide by the law, you know," he said self-righteously as he walked away.

Soon everyone knew about the greedy ways of Xiao-Bo who wanted money for everything. He never once gave anything away. He always demanded payment for everything, no matter how trivial it was.

"It's the law, you know," he would say, sounding very wise and knowledgeable. "You have to obey the law at all times."

Now, outside Xiao-Bo's house grew a very large cypress tree. Xiao-Bo had planted it many years ago. It had grown tall and handsome and its branches spread far and wide, giving cool shade over a large area.

One hot afternoon, a tired traveller stopped under his tree to rest. It was so cool and comfortable in the shade that he fell asleep. When he awoke, he saw Xiao-Bo standing over him, looking very stern.

"You have been resting in the shade of a tree that belongs to me," said Xiao-Bo. "The tree and its shade are mine. You must pay me for having used what is mine."

"But this tree is outside your house! Surely its shade is for everybody," said the traveller, a young man.

"It is my tree and my shade," persisted Xiao-Bo. "You must pay for my shade if you want to use it!"

The traveller thought this over for a while. At last he said, "All right, I'm going to buy the shade of your tree."

Xiao-Bo's eyes glittered greedily. He could even sell the shade of his cypress tree! The young man looked as if he came from a rich family so Xiao-Bo quoted a high price. The young man took out a cloth bag from around his waist and paid immediately.

Xiao-Bo was full of good humour as he counted the silver coins and put them into his pocket. "What a fine young man you are!" he said, his fat, oily face beaming with pleasure. "Now you own the shade of my cypress tree and you and your friends can rest in it anytime you like! I shall not stop you, for you have paid for it. It's the law, you know!"

"Yes, according to the law, I own the shade of your tree now," said the young man, smiling.

"Yes, yes," agreed Xiao-Bo. "As you have paid for the shade, it is yours as well as whatever lies in the shade. These cypress leaves now lying in the shade are yours!"

The next morning, Xiao-Bo was astonished to find the young man and six of his friends inside his compound, near his plum trees. They were lying on the ground, resting comfortably and eating his plums.

"Hey, what are you doing here?" demanded Xiao-Bo angrily. "Why are you eating my plums?"

"We're resting in the shade which belongs to me,"

said the young man. "And we're eating the plums because they too belong to me. They happen to be in my shade so they are mine. Remember our agreement."

Indeed, at that time of day, the shadow of the cypress tree fell inside the landlord's compound and shaded the short plum trees.

"Wh . . . what, why . . . " stuttered the landlord, but he couldn't do anything. According to the agreement, the shade and the plums belonged to the young man.

In the late afternoon, the young man and his friends followed the shade and established themselves comfortably inside the landlord's house! There were now ten people altogether for the young man had invited more friends. They sat on the landlord's silk cushions and lay on the carpet on his floor. The young man settled himself comfortably in the landlord's favourite chair and fell asleep, snoring loudly.

Xiao-Bo stared at them angrily, but he could do nothing. At that particular time, the shadow of his cypress tree happened to fall over the house, over his lovely furniture and they all now belonged to the young man because that was part of the agreement!

It grieved Xiao-Bo to see so many people in his house making use of his things, but he could only stare helplessly.

Later, with the movement of the sun, the shadow of the cypress tree fell on Xiao-Bo's bedroom. The young man and his friends trooped into the room. Now there were thirty of them, for the young man had invited many more. They made themselves comfortable on Xiao-Bo's bed, his soft silk cushions, his cool polished floors. These belonged to the young man now!

"Hey, what's this under the bed?" said the young man, drawing out a large wooden chest. He opened it. It was full of silver coins! "Ah, it belongs to me now, because it's in the shade which I bought," he said happily.

Xiao-Bo protested wildly. "No, no, no!" he cried in distress. "You can't take away my silver! It's mine!"

"Ah, have you forgotten our agreement?" asked the young man. "You mustn't go against the law, you know."

So the young man and his friends managed to take a

lot of valuable things, as well as the chest of silver coins, out of Xiao-Bo's house.

Although from another part of the country, the young man had heard of how the greedy landlord squeezed money out of even the very poor people. He now called all those who had been bullied by Xiao-Bo to come forward and he distributed Xiao-Bo's valuables and silver coins among them. They went away with happy smiles on their faces.

As for Xiao-Bo, he packed up and left for another part of the country. You may be sure nobody missed him!

THE TRANSFORMATION OF THE MOUNTAIN LION

THE PEOPLE IN THE little village of Zhang, which lay at the foot of a tall mountain, were filled with terror. A large lion, a ferocious beast, frequently came down from its mountain cave to terrorise the villagers. It had already killed many cows, sheep, goats and pigs. It had even killed a few people. This mountain lion, which was said to be so huge and powerful that no human being could subdue it, became the terror of the villagers of Zhang.

At last, unable to bear the killings anymore, they organised a large party to go up the mountain to kill this dreaded beast. The party comprised strong men, armed with knives, axes, poles and ropes. They waited outside the lion's cave, but strangely, there was no sign of the animal. They waited for several days, but still no lion appeared. Discouraged, the men returned to their village.

Determined to hunt down the mountain lion, the villagers decided to consult their great teacher, Lao Tzu, who was full of wisdom. They called out to him, for this great one lived in the heavens and sometimes came down to earth in a bright chariot.

As they called, a black cloud gathered over the village and descended slowly earthwards. As soon as it touched the ground, it burst into a bright light. From this light stepped the great Lao Tzu.

The villagers told their teacher of the cause of their troubles and begged him to help them capture the mountain lion.

Lao Tzu listened carefully and then said, "The real trouble is that you do not understand this mountain lion. I shall help you, but first, I shall need one of you to assist me."

A strong and handsome young man named Yung stepped forward and volunteered to help.

"Now let me have a kid," said Lao Tzu.

One of the villagers, a farmer who owned several goats, went to bring a kid. They thought that Lao Tzu was going to use the little kid to trap the mountain lion.

"Now we must be off to the mountain lion's cave," said Lao Tzu. He went, followed by Yung carrying the kid, and the villagers. However, before they reached the mountain lion's cave, Lao Tzu told the villagers to return home, as only he and Yung would go into the lion's cave.

Entering the cave, they saw the bones of animals scattered around. In a corner of the cave was a bed of sand. Lao Tzu instructed Yung to place the little kid on the bed of sand.

"Poor little thing," thought Yung, as he gently lay the small creature on the sand. "It will soon be devoured by that terrible beast."

The little kid curled up on the sand and was soon fast asleep.

"Now we shall hide behind the rocks outside the

cave and wait for the lion," said Lao Tzu.

They did not have to wait long for the beast to appear. It came, a huge, ferocious-looking creature, carrying a dead deer in its mouth. As it reached the entrance of its cave, it paused suddenly, having smelt another animal. Dropping the deer, it moved forward menacingly. Soon it discovered the little kid sleeping on the sand in a corner of the cave.

"Oh, it's going to kill the poor little innocent thing!" thought Yung, his heart filled with pity.

He closed his eyes and when he opened them again, he was astonished to see the lion licking the kid in a most affectionate manner! The kid was awake now and was making little bleating noises which seemed to pacify and please the lion. It continued to sniff, lick and nuzzle the little creature.

The kid got up and began to play with the lion. Together, the two animals rolled and tumbled on the floor in great playfulness. When they were tired of playing, they lay down and went to sleep, the little kid snugly curled up against the lion's great body.

What an amazing sight! Lao Tzu and Yung, tired with their waiting and watching, also fell asleep. When they awoke, they could no longer see the lion and the kid. Yung was alarmed.

"Master! Master!" he said. "The lion has run off! We have failed to kill him!"

"Kill him?" said Lao Tzu. "Come and see."

He led Yung to a grassy slope a short distance from the cave. Here, they saw the lion resting near a mound while the little kid nibbled the grass near by. The lion appeared to be keeping careful watch on the little creature, like a mother taking care of her child. To Yung, the lion's eyes appeared to be filled with love for the little one.

"All is well," said Lao Tzu. "A little innocent kid has tamed the ferocious lion. Its savage instincts have been replaced by love and gentleness. Let us now return."

At the foot of the mountain they saw a black cloud over their heads. The cloud became larger as it descended towards earth. Touching earth, it burst into bright light. A beautiful cloud chariot appeared and Lao Tzu stepped into it.

"I shall return in six months," he said, as he was borne aloft in the chariot.

Yung returned to the village and told the villagers what had happened. Some, however, did not really believe him.

About three months later, Yung decided to go by himself to the mountain lion's cave to see if anything had happened. He saw the kid, now grown bigger, prancing happily about in the cave. He looked around for the lion and could hardly believe what he saw.

The lion was now half human! It still kept its lion's head but the body was that of a man! Yung stared. He watched while the lion caressed the kid and lay down to sleep with it on the bed of sand. Returning to the village, Yung wondered whether the villagers would believe him.

As soon as he reached the village, someone told him breathlessly, "A very strange thing happened yesterday. Old widow Chao was gathering firewood when a snake suddenly appeared. It was about to strike at the old woman when a strange creature — half lion, half man — appeared and killed it! This mysterious creature then helped the frightened woman to her feet and led her out of the forest. She said it had the kindest, gentlest look in the world!"

Yung, after listening to this account, exclaimed, "It is the mountain lion! Love has transformed it and changed its savage nature. Even its body has become human!"

Three months later, just as he had promised, Lao Tzu revisited the village. When Yung and the others told him of the transformation of the mountain lion, he smiled and said, "All is well now. There is no more need to fear the mountain lion. It has been transformed by love and you too, all of you, have been transformed by love that is working in your midst."

As he was talking, he turned in the direction of the mountain. A young man, tall and handsome, was walking towards the group. Everyone knew who he was — the mountain lion fully changed into a human being.

The young man approached Lao Tzu and knelt before him. Lao Tzu invited him to enter the chariot. Then, as the villagers watched, their faces shining with wonder, the chariot slowly ascended into the sky, surrounded by a blaze of brilliant light.

THREE GIFTS FROM THE GREEN DRAGON

THERE WAS ONCE A very simple-minded young man in a small village in China. Although he was already twenty years old, he had the mind of a child. Everybody in the village called him Gong-Gong which means "ignorant" or "silly".

His mother was in despair, for she wanted him to be like her other two sons who were sharp and clever. Gong-Gong's elder brothers were always making fun of him.

"You'll never come to any good," sneered his first brother.

"You'll spend your whole life making people laugh at you," jeered his second brother.

One day, Gong-Gong's mother made some delicious rice dumplings. She covered them carefully with a large leaf and gave them to her son, saying, "My son, go away from this village and seek your fortune elsewhere in this wide world. Here's some food for your journey."

Gong-Gong took the rice dumplings and cheerfully started out on his way. As he was passing a forest, he saw a green snake. The snake appeared thin and hungry. Gong-Gong felt sorry for it. He opened the package containing the rice dumplings his mother had made for him. "Here, eat this, you poor starving snake," said the kind-hearted Gong-Gong.

The snake gobbled up the rice dumplings greedily. It ate and ate until the last rice dumpling was gone. Then something happened to the snake. It grew bigger and bigger!

It said to Gong-Gong, "Quick, put me into the large pond that you will find on the edge of this forest."

So Gong-Gong carried the snake, which was now quite huge, and carefully put it into the pond which was very large and deep. The snake grew even bigger and then, suddenly, lo! It became a huge, green dragon!

The dragon said to Gong-Gong, "I must reward you for your kindness to me. Turn around and you'll see something."

Gong-Gong turned around and saw a donkey.

"Now ask the donkey in a loud voice what it can do," said the dragon.

Gong-Gong asked the animal in a loud, clear voice, "Donkey, donkey, what can you do?"

At once, the donkey opened its mouth and out fell a heap of gold coins! Gong-Gong grinned with pleasure.

"The donkey is yours. Now continue on your journey," said the dragon.

Gong-Gong sat on the donkey and went on his way. As night fell, he came to an inn.

The innkeeper, a fat man with small greedy eyes, looked at Gong-Gong's humble clothes and said haughtily, "There's no place at my inn for people who cannot pay well."

"But I can pay you!" cried Gong-Gong. He leapt down from the donkey's back and cried, "Donkey, donkey, what can you do?"

The donkey opened its mouth, and to the astonishment of the innkeeper, gold coins poured out on to the ground. He greedily scooped up the gold coins with his fat hands. He gave Gong-Gong a comfortable room in his inn and tethered the donkey in the yard.

In the middle of the night, the innkeeper stole out into the yard. He untethered the donkey and replaced it with one of his own, which looked very much like Gong-Gong's. Then, with a crafty smile, he took Gong-Gong's donkey into the house and kept it in a secret room.

The next morning, Gong-Gong prepared to leave. Of course, he had no idea of what the innkeeper had done. He mounted his donkey and said cheerfully, "We're going home! We'll give Mother a nice surprise!"

Soon Gong-Gong reached his village. He announced cheerfully, "Mother, Elder Brothers, come and see something wonderful!"

Gong-Gong's mother, two brothers and the neighbours ran out in surprise and crowded around him and the donkey, eager to see what he was going to show them. Gong-Gong jumped down from the donkey and said in a loud voice, "Donkey, donkey, what can you do?"

The donkey merely looked sleepily at him and flicked its tail at a passing fly.

"Well?" said the onlookers. "What is it supposed to do?"

"It's supposed to open its mouth for gold coins to fall out!" cried Gong-Gong, looking very upset.

"Ha, ha, ha, ha, ha!" laughed the elder brothers, and they laughed so much that they rolled helplessly on the ground, clutching each other.

"Gong-Gong, come into the house and have something to eat. You are talking nonsense because you are hungry," said his mother, shaking her head.

Poor Gong-Gong couldn't understand it.

The next morning, he rode away on his donkey and came to the pond where the green dragon was.

He looked so sad that the green dragon came up from the pond and said, "Never mind, Gong-Gong. Turn around and you'll see something."

Gong-Gong turned around and saw a red cotton tablecloth.

"Now ask the tablecloth what it can do," said the dragon.

"Tablecloth, tablecloth, what can you do?" asked Gong-Gong.

Immediately, the tablecloth spread itself on the ground and lo and behold! On it was the most delicious-looking food that Gong-Gong had ever seen! There were bowls of steaming hot soup, plates of meat cooked with rare spices and vegetables, and cakes and puddings made from the finest rice flour and covered with coloured sugar!

Gong-Gong's eyes opened in wonder. Looking at all this delicious food, he felt quite hungry. He sat down and had a hearty meal.

"The tablecloth is yours," said the green dragon and disappeared back into its pond.

Gong-Gong rolled up the wonderful tablecloth and once more made his way to the inn.

The greedy innkeeper came out and said haughtily, "If you have come for a meal, it's too late. I'm getting ready to go to bed."

"Oh no, I don't need anyone to cook for me!" cried Gong-Gong. He unrolled the tablecloth and cried loudly, "Tablecloth, tablecloth, what can you do?"

At once, the tablecloth spread itself, and on it appeared the most sumptious meal the innkeeper had ever seen. Even the innkeeper's wife, who was the best cook in the country, couldn't prepare a meal like that. The greedy innkeeper sat down and helped himself to as much of the food as he could.

That night, as Gong-Gong slept, the evil man stole into his room, quietly removed the rolled tablecloth near Gong-Gong's sleeping form and replaced it with a tablecloth exactly like it.

The next morning, Gong-Gong set out for home. This time, he thought happily, he could not fail to give his mother and brothers a surprise. Whistling merrily, Gong-Gong came to his village.

"Mother, Elder Brothers, I have a surprise for you!" he called. They came out and crowded around him.

"Call the neighbours! They can share in the surprise," said Gong-Gong.

He took the rolled tablecloth from under his arm and called out in a loud voice, "Tablecloth, tablecloth, what can you do?"

The tablecloth remained in its rolled state. Nothing happened.

"Now what kind of foolish joke is this?" cried the onlookers.

"It's supposed to spread out and give us a big delicious meal," cried Gong-Gong, looking very upset. "It can produce tasty soups, meat fried with ginger strips, steamed vegetables . . . "

"Ha, ha, ha, ha, ha!" roared the brothers, slapping their thighs in their enjoyment of Gong-Gong's stupidity.

"Gong-Gong, you must be very hungry. Come inside and I'll get you something to eat," said his mother wearily.

Poor Gong-Gong was most distressed.

The next morning he went to the pond of the green dragon again.

The green dragon said, "Gong-Gong, turn around and you'll see something."

Gong-Gong turned around and saw a large stick, long and stout and so well polished that it gleamed.

"Don't ask it what it can do," said the dragon as it disappeared into the pond.

Gong-Gong took the stick and went to the inn.

"Ha! What is this?" asked the innkeeper, looking at the stick curiously.

"Don't ask it what it can do," said Gong-Gong.

That night, the innkeeper gave Gong-Gong a good meal and a comfortable room so that he would sleep soundly. In the middle of the night, he stole into the room. He looked at the stick with greedy eyes.

"Now what shall I get this time?" he thought greedily.

He cried, "Stick, stick, what can you do?" Immediately the stick flew high up into the air and came down heavily upon the back of the innkeeper!

THWACK! THWACK! The stick first beat his back, then his head, then his legs, then his back again.

THWACK! THWACK!

"Help! Help!" cried the innkeeper.

He ran here and there, but the stick followed him and continued to beat vigorously. It was a stout stick and it seemed to enjoy beating the innkeeper. THWACK! THWACK!

"Stop it, stop it, someone!" moaned the innkeeper.

Gong-Gong was awake by this time. He stared in amazement on seeing the stick beating the innkeeper.

"Ouch!" the man yelled as the stick hit both legs. At last he could not stand it anymore. "Stop it," he cried to Gong-Gong, "I promise to give you back your

donkey and your tablecloth."

Gong-Gong said "Stop!" to the stick.

Immediately, it dropped to the ground.

Covered with bruises, the innkeeper went to bring the donkey and the tablecloth. He returned them to Gong-Gong, promising never to steal anything again.

With his donkey, tablecloth and stick, Gong-Gong went back once more to his village.

This time, the two elder brothers refused to come out of the house when Gong-Gong called. Gong-Gong's mother and some neighbours gathered round.

"Donkey, donkey, what can you do?" cried Gong-Gong in a loud voice.

At once the donkey opened its mouth and glittering gold coins poured out. Those who were looking on screamed with delight.

Gong-Gong then said to the tablecloth, "Table-cloth, tablecloth, what can you do?"

Immediately, the tablecloth spread itself on the floor, and on it appeared the most tantalising dishes that anybody had ever seen! All sat down and had the most delicious meal in their lives.

The two brothers who had been watching all this in amazement from inside the house now ran out. They rudely pushed the others aside so that they could have the best dishes and they even forced the neighbours to give them the gold pieces.

"Stick, stick, what can you do?" cried Gong-Gong, very displeased by his brothers' rude behaviour.

The stick flew into the air and came down heavily first on First Brother's head and then on Second Brother's back. THWACK! THWACK!

"Ouch! Stop it!" cried the brothers.

"Will you learn to behave?" cried Gong-Gong.

"Yes, we will," said the brothers tearfully.

So, with his marvellous donkey, tablecloth and stick, Gong-Gong lived a happy life in his village, helping all those who needed his help. He showed so much wisdom and kindness in his dealings with people that he was later chosen to be the leader and adviser of the villagers. Of course, nobody ever called him "Gong-Gong" again.

IN FATHER'S FOOTSTEPS

HAN ZI WAS SAID to be the brightest little boy in his village, and indeed he was. He was only six years old, but he was always asking questions.

Sometimes his questions made the adults in the village laugh. Once, for instance, Han Zi wanted to know why the old farmer Ji Bao had, on his chin, a black mole with five hairs and why Ji Bao's wife never smiled. Another day, Han Zi asked why the moon came out at night only and why Su Dai, the woman who kept pigs, cried when one of her pigs died.

Sometimes, the adults gave in to little Han Zi's questions and told him correct answers in quite a serious manner, treating him as if he were an adult like themselves. Han Zi always listened very carefully to what the adults told him. He stored up all the information and advice given him in his little mind and thought about it as he lay on his mat at night, just before falling off to sleep.

Han Zi lived with his parents and grandfather in a little thatched hut, on the edge of a rice field. His father, Guan Zhong, was a farmer. He worked very hard on his rice field. The rice field was divided into small plots and on the little strips of land separating the plots, Guan Zhong planted vegetables and fruits.

Guan Zhong was very careful about making use of every square inch of land he possessed. He did not believe in waste of any kind, and whatever he had, he put to full use, whether it was his land, the water from his well or the manure from the droppings of his pigs and oxen.

Few farmers worked as hard as Guan Zhong. He expected others to work hard also and scolded his wife and old father if they did not do enough work on the farm. He was impatient with those who were lazy or useless, and showed his scorn for those neighbours who did not work as hard as he did.

Even little Han Zi was expected to do his share of the work. His father took him out to the rice field or the vegetable plots and told him to help water the vegetables, to pull out the useless weeds that choked the growing rice plants or to take care of the chickens and ducks and see that no one came to steal them.

"You must work hard like me," Guan Zhong would tell his son. "You must follow in your father's footsteps."

Han Zi would listen very carefully, his large eyes fixed on his father's face.

Once, Han Zi gave one of the small rice cakes his mother had made to an old beggar who was passing through the village. He felt sorry for the beggar and ran into the house to take one of the rice cakes for him. When Guan Zhong was told of this by his wife, he was rather displeased with his son.

"In future, you must not waste food," he said severely. "You must be careful like me. Have you ever seen me being wasteful in any way? Always remember to follow in your father's footsteps."

"Yes, Father," said Han Zi obediently. He was sorry he had displeased his father and was determined not to behave in the same way in future.

Han Zi was rather afraid of his father but not so of his grandfather. He was always asking the old man questions.

"Grandfather, Grandfather, why is your hair all white?" asked Han Zi one day.

"Because I'm a very old man. When you reach my age, you will have white hair too," said Grandfather, chuckling a little.

"Grandfather, why are there wrinkles on your face?" asked Han Zi, staring at the many furrows on the old man's forehead and cheeks.

"Why, because I'm a very old man!" laughed Grandfather.

"Grandfather, why are you so thin? Your arms and legs are like sticks!" cried Han Zi.

Now this question the old man was reluctant to answer, for it would bring tears to his old eyes. He was thin and weak because his son Guan Zhong did not give him enough food. He had only a small bowl of rice for his meal each day.

Guan Zhong had given instructions to his wife not

to let the old man have more than this amount of food. The reason was that Guan Zhong's father was nearly eighty years old, and was no longer capable of doing any work on the farm or in the house. His eyesight was too poor, his steps were too slow, his muscles were too weak. Therefore, Guan Zhong argued, he was now useless and did not deserve the food he was eating and the shelter he was getting. Guan Zhong's heart was as hard as steel, and he was never touched by pity at the sight of a hungry, old man, even though the old man was his own father.

Indeed, he grudged his father even the small bowl of rice he was given daily. To make sure that the "useless old man" did not get more than he deserved, he gave instructions that his rice was to be ladled into a special bowl. This bowl was much smaller in size than the other bowls in the house! It was old and chipped and stained, but that did not bother Guan Zhong. Han Zi knew that only this bowl was to be used by his grandfather. The old man always ate up every grain of rice in his bowl, but nobody was allowed to give him more.

Besides food, Guan Zhong was grudging in the provision of bedding for the old man. He provided an old, tattered mat which was unrolled in a dark corner of the house for the old man to sleep on at night. The thin mat did not prevent the hardness or the cold of the floor from hurting the old man's body. Still there was nothing he could do. Every night, he curled to sleep on the old mat, hungry, cold and miserable.

Han Zi watched him with wide-open eyes, his active little mind full of questions which he did not dare ask.

Guan Zhong, however, was by no means satisfied. He still believed that he was doing too much for the old man who he felt was absolutely useless.

"Why should he continue to stay in my house and eat my food when he is incapable of doing anything useful?" Guan Zhong muttered to his wife. "He has become such a burden!"

A plan began to form in the heartless Guan Zhong's mind. He would get rid of his old father! He would make a basket, a large reed basket, and he would put the old man in it and carry him into the dark forest one night. He would then leave the old one there — he did not care whether the old man would be killed by beasts or die of starvation.

Guan Zhong went down to the river's edge where plenty of reeds grew and cut as many as he could carry. Back home, he began to make the basket with his wife's help.

Han Zi watched his father's skilful fingers plaiting the soft reeds and asked what it was for.

"To make a large basket to carry your grandfather into the forest," replied Guan Zhong in a businesslike tone. "He's absolutely useless now in his old age, and I don't want him around anymore!"

"Yes, Father," said Han Zi meekly, looking with wide eyes upon the basket taking shape. In a day or two the basket would be ready.

On the evening that Guan Zhong was planning to put his old father into the basket and carry him off into the dark forest, he saw little Han Zi at the back of the house, very busy at work on something. There was a large pile of river reeds in front of the boy who was sitting on the ground.

"What are you doing, Han Zi?" demanded his father.

"I'm trying to weave a basket out of these reeds,

Father, just like you," replied Han Zi.

Guan Zhong was quite pleased. The basket, if well woven, could be sold at the market. Then he looked closer and saw a small, brown bowl and a tattered mat beside his son.

"What are these?" he demanded again, pointing.

"I'm saving all these up, Father," said Han Zi.

"Saving up? Whatever are you talking about, son?" asked Guan Zhong sternly.

"Mother told me to throw away Grandfather's rice bowl and mat," said Han Zi. "But that would be wasteful. You've always told me not to be wasteful,

Father, and I would like to follow in your footsteps. I'm making this basket from the reeds left over from the basket you made for Grandfather. I shall need the basket, bowl and mat for you in your old age."

Guan Zhong stared. He turned white. His mouth opened but he did not know what to say.

THE MAGIC BUCKWHEAT PANCAKES

IN WESTERN CHINA, long ago, a lady who was known only as "Third Lady" owned an inn by the side of a road. The inn was very popular with travellers, for there was always plenty to eat and drink and the rooms were very comfortable. The most attractive thing about the inn was the low charge for the rooms and food.

Nobody knew how Third Lady happened to have such a name. Indeed, nobody knew anything about her, who her family was or where she had come from. She never spoke to anyone about herself, but was on friendly terms with all. She always smiled at her visitors and did her best to make them feel comfortable.

She explained that she was able to afford the low charges for the rooms at her inn and for the food because she had another business which brought in sufficient money. This business was trade in donkeys. What a strange business for a lady! But, of course, the visitors to the inn were too polite to comment on this.

At the back of the inn was a long row of stalls which Third Lady had built for her donkeys. The donkeys

always looked strong and healthy. One evening, a travelling scholar named Chao stopped at Third Lady's inn. He was very tired after a long journey, and Third Lady immediately made him feel welcome. She gave him a room next to her own.

There were four other guests who arrived at about the same time as Chao. They were strong, healthy young men. Third Lady welcomed them warmly. Then she bade them all sit down, and brought them large goblets of wine. Chao was not in the habit of drinking wine and politely refused. The others drank heartily and afterwards felt very sleepy. They all then retired to their rooms and slept soundly.

Chao, however, did not go to sleep immediately. At midnight, he heard strange noises coming from Third Lady's room which was next to his.

Putting his eye to a little crack in the wooden wall separating the rooms, Chao saw something that made him gasp in astonishment. It was the strangest thing he had ever seen.

He saw Third Lady go to a hole in the brick wall on the opposite side of the room. She drew out a wooden box and, kneeling on the floor, carefully opened it. Inside were tiny wooden figures. Third Lady took these out and stood them on the carpet. Then she blew three times on them, and as if by magic, all the little wooden figures came to life!

Chao could hardly believe his eyes. As he continued to watch through the crack, he saw that the little wooden men were getting ready to do something. One scattered dirt on the carpet. Two drew wooden ploughs back and forth over the dirt, making tiny furrows. A third, who was carrying a little sack of buckwheat seeds, scattered them in the furrows.

Almost immediately, tiny buckwheat plants sprouted and ripened quickly. Two of the little men ground the grain into flour. They did it so thoroughly that the flour was as fine as powder. They put the flour into little sacks and handed these to Third Lady, who was looking on smilingly at all that was going on.

"My little servants, thank you!" cried Third Lady. "Now it is time for you to take your rest!"

The wooden men lined up on the edge of the carpet. Third Lady blew three times on them. Instantly, they became lifeless wooden figures again. Third Lady then put them back into the box and returned the box to its place in the hole in the wall.

"Ah, now to bake some buckwheat pancakes!" cried Third Lady, looking very pleased with herself.

Chao could hardly get over his astonishment. What strange happenings were taking place in the inn! What a mysterious person Third Lady was! Chao began to get suspicious. Was she planning to do something evil? He determined to watch her very carefully.

The next morning, Chao sat with the other guests at the table, waiting for breakfast. Third Lady came in, bearing a plate of freshly made buckwheat pancakes. How delicious they looked and smelt!

"Ah, here are buckwheat pancakes for breakfast!" cried Third Lady. "I'm sure you'll enjoy them."

The four guests looked eagerly at the steaming pancakes on the plate.

Chao, however, was determined not to touch them. With great presence of mind, he suddenly got up, saying with pretended agitation, "I forgot I must rush off this morning! I have some urgent business to attend to, but I shall be back this evening!" With that, he rushed out of the inn.

However, he did not go far. As soon as he was outside, he silently stole up to a window from which he could peep into the room. He peeped and saw yet more strange things. As soon as the four guests had swallowed the first mouthful of the buckwheat pancakes, they changed into donkeys! Great, big, healthy donkeys!

"Ha, ha, ha!" laughed Third Lady. "Four more

donkeys for sale," she said, as she took them out to the donkey stalls at the back of the inn. "That will fetch a nice sum!"

Chao determined to do something to punish Third Lady who was obviously an enchantress or witch in human form.

He went down and bought some buckwheat pancakes from a village tavern. They were very much like

Third Lady's pancakes in size and texture. Carefully wrapping the pancakes in his handkerchief, he put them into his pocket and returned to Third Lady's inn.

"Ah, you are back!" she cried in a friendly voice. "You must not fail to taste my lovely buckwheat pancakes tomorrow."

"Where are the four guests?" inquired Chao. "I thought they were staying for a few days."

"Oh, they decided to leave after breakfast. They said they had some business to attend to in town," said Third Lady sweetly.

Next morning, as Chao sat at the table, she brought in a plate of steaming buckwheat pancakes. They really smelt delicious. Third Lady put three on Chao's plate and three on her own. Chao was certain the pancakes she had put on her own plate were ordinary ones.

At that moment a guest arrived and Third Lady went off to see and welcome him. Chao grabbed the opportunity to take three buckwheat pancakes from his pocket and put them on his plate. Quickly he removed the three pancakes from Third Lady's plate, hid them in his pocket and replaced these with the three that Third Lady had given him. Then he sat and waited for Third Lady to return.

"Ah, I see you've not touched the pancakes!" she cried when she came in. "Aren't they good enough for you?"

"Madam, I shall be pleased if you will join me for breakfast," said Chao politely. "Oh, of course!" cried Third Lady gaily. She took one of the pancakes that Chao had put on her plate and bit into it.

She swallowed a mouthful and — hey presto! Third

Lady changed into a donkey! Since she was a large woman, the donkey was big and strong. It began to bray and kick its legs about.

"Ah, Third Lady, how does it feel to be a donkey?" cried Chao. "I saw how your magic buckwheat cakes were made, and how the four poor young men changed into donkeys after they had eaten them!"

Chao was anxious to know how to change all the earlier guests from their donkey form back into men. They were a sorry sight as they stood in their stalls, braying mournfully. He decided to seek the advice of a wise old man who lived in a temple on a remote hill. He rode there on Third-Lady-turned-donkey, talking to her severely all the time about her wicked deeds.

The wise old man told Chao, "I know this woman. She is an enchantress. The only way to get rid of her power and to rescue those poor unfortunate men who have been turned into donkeys, is to destroy those magic beings who do her bidding!"

"I know! The box with the little wooden figures!" cried Chao excitedly. He rode back to the inn, found the box and, going to the edge of a very deep lake, flung it into the water. It sank to the bottom of the lake.

At once, all the donkeys were changed back into human beings again! Great was their wonder as they looked at each other. They could not thank the scholar Chao enough for what he had done for them.

As for Third Lady, she too changed back to human form when the wooden box was thrown into the lake. Knowing that she was exposed and all her power gone, she ran off into the dark forest and nobody ever saw or heard of her again.

THE GIRL
WITH THE WARTS

IN A MOUNTAIN village in China, a very long time ago, there lived a man whose wife died soon after the birth of her baby girl. The man was filled with sorrow, but he married again soon after, for the sake of his baby daughter whom he named Yin-Fei. He wanted someone to love and care for Yin-Fei and to take the place of her dead mother.

Alas, the woman he married, a widow with a little daughter of her own, was sly and evil-hearted. While the man lived, she pretended to be very good to Yin-Fei, but the moment he died, she ill-treated the girl openly. Yin-Fei was then only twelve.

Yin-Fei's stepmother and stepsister, Yu-Wen, disliked her so much that they did everything to make life miserable for her.

"Yin-Fei! Get up, lazybones, the cock has crowed," her stepmother would call out shrilly.

"Yin-Fei, my dress must be washed, my slippers cleaned, and my hair-comb prepared for my visit to Aunt's next week," Yu-Wen would say.

"Yin-Fei, you good-for-nothing! You've burnt the bean soup again!" her stepmother would scold.

"Yin-Fei, there's no need to look into the mirror. Everybody knows how ugly you are!" Yu-Wen would say spitefully.

Now this was not true at all, for Yin-Fei was growing up to be a very beautiful girl. Yu-Wen, who was not as pretty, was dreadfully jealous and showed her jealousy by spiteful words and actions. She was angry because Yin-Fei's skin was smoother and whiter, Yin-Fei's hair was softer and more lustrous and her eyes and mouth were more delicately shaped. Everybody in the village remarked on Yin-Fei's growing beauty and that made Yu-Wen furious. She was good-looking, but beside Yin-Fei she appeared plain and ordinary.

Her mother, who loved her very much, disliked to hear anyone comparing the looks of the two girls. She gave the best clothes to her own daughter and bought flowers and ornaments for her hair. For Yin-Fei, there were only cast-off clothes and slippers. Despite this, Yin-Fei far outshone her stepsister in beauty.

One day, while Yin-Fei was out of the house tending to the chickens, her stepmother and stepsister had an unusual visitor. The visitor was a very ugly woman, whom they had never met before. The reason for her ugliness was a big, black wart on her face. She asked for a drink of water and then began to tell them how she came to have such a terrible appearance.

"There was a large bush in the forest not far from here," she said sadly. "The bush was full of bright, red, juicy berries. I plucked a few and ate them — stupid me! And see what happened to me!" She began to cry. The wart really made her look hideous.

"Will you be able to show us this bush?" cried mother and daughter together, for an evil plan was forming in their minds simultaneously.

"Yes, but I advise you to stay as far away from it as possible," said the ugly woman.

When shown the bush, Yu-Wen and her mother immediately picked a large handful of the berries. During the night, while Yin-Fei was asleep, they squeezed out the juice of the berries. The next morning, they secretly put the juice in Yin-Fei's food.

Suspecting nothing, Yin-Fei ate her bowl of rice, fish and vegetables. A short while later, ugly warts appeared. There was one big black one on her forehead, two large reddish ones on her right cheek, and a whole cluster of smaller ones on her left cheek. There were even several huge ones on her neck.

Poor Yin-Fei was shocked. She did not know what was happening. She stared at herself in the mirror, and wept in horror. How ugly she had become! The delicacy of her skin and features was destroyed by the presence of so many large, black or reddish warts. Yin-Fei sobbed bitterly.

Yu-Wen and her mother secretly chuckled in glee. Now who could say that Yin-Fei was more beautiful than Yu-Wen? The two evil women had never felt so happy in their lives.

Yin-Fei kept to the house, not daring to go out for

fear that people would stare and laugh at her. She was utterly miserable. She only went out at night, taking long walks in the forest, to try to forget her misery.

One evening, as she was walking through the forest, she suddenly realised that she had wandered into a part that was totally unfamiliar to her. She walked on and on in the dark, not knowing where she was going and becoming more and more frightened.

Suddenly, she saw a light in the distance. Approaching it, she realised that it was coming from a cave. The cave appeared to be warm and brilliantly lit and she quickly walked towards it. Feeling very tired and hungry as she entered it, she hoped to meet someone kind who would offer her shelter and food.

To her astonishment and dismay, a group of strange creatures emerged from various parts of the cave to look at her. They looked very strange indeed. They looked like human beings, yet were not completely so. Their skin was rough, their features coarse and when they opened their mouths to speak to one another, their voices were rough.

Yin-Fei suddenly remembered something. When she was a little girl, her father used to tell her stories of the strange creatures which lived in the forests and mountains. One group of these creatures was called the Rough People, because they looked like people but had very rough skin, rough voices and rough ways. These creatures were also very simple-minded and shy, so they kept away from the outside world. They had magical powers and possessed vast wealth in the form of diamonds, rubies, emeralds and other precious stones.

Yin-Fei was frightened as she stood surrounded by the Rough People. Determined not to show her fear,

however, she began to sing. Her voice trembled a little at first but as she went on singing, delightful flute-like sounds filled the cave. To Yin-Fei's relief, she saw the looks of annoyance on the faces of the Rough People disappear. They now looked very pleased.

The leader of the group stepped up to Yin-Fei and said, in a voice that was very rough, "Where did those sounds come from? We want to make sounds like those too!"

"Why, from my throat!" cried Yin-Fei, surprised that the Rough People did not know where a voice came from.

"That cannot be," said the leader abruptly. "Look, we have throats too but we cannot make sounds like those. They must come from somewhere else!"

Yin-Fei did not know what to say to that.

Suddenly, one of the Rough People who had been looking hard at Yin-Fei said, "I know, I know! The sounds come from those things on her face and neck! Those are the only things she has that we do not. The sounds must come from there!"

The others became excited at the discovery and crowded round to look closely at the warts on Yin-Fei's face and neck.

"Will you give us those things in exchange for some of these?" asked the leader, pointing to a sack of something in the corner of the cave. The sack was full of sparkling diamonds, gold coins, jade, and rubies!

"It's no use," said Yin-Fei sadly. "I would give you these horrible things for free but they cannot be removed. They will always remain on my face and neck to make me miserable."

"Ah, you leave that to me," said the leader.

He told Yin-Fei to close her eyes. She did as she was told. On opening them again, she saw to her utter amazement that the warts had all left her face and were in the hands of the leader! Thinking she was dreaming, Yin-Fei lifted her hands to feel her face and neck. Yes, the warts had all disappeared! Her skin was as smooth as before. Yin-Fei's heart sang for joy.

Before she left the cave, the leader gave her a handful of precious stones, one for each of the warts he had taken from her face and neck! Yin-Fei left hurriedly. Clutching the precious stones in her hand, she managed to stumble out of the forest in the darkness. What thrilled her most was the fact that she had regained her beauty.

When she reached home, she related her strange experiences to her stepmother and stepsister. They were secretly filled with anger to see her beautiful once more. What made them even angrier was that with the precious stones she was now richer than them.

That night, Yu-Wen and her mother had a secret discussion. Yu-Wen's eyes lit up as she told her mother of her plan. It was easy, she said. She would obtain the berries from the bush in the forest, eat them, get as many warts as possible and then exchange them for precious stones from the stupid creatures in the cave!

Yu-Wen and her mother were so excited about the plan that they began to work on it immediately. They brought back a large handful of the berries from the forest and Yu-Wen quickly ate every one of them. The warts appeared instantly on her forehead, cheeks, nose and neck. Neither Yu-Wen nor her mother, however, was alarmed.

That night, Yu-Wen stole out of the house and walked towards the dark forest. She found the cave of the Rough People without difficulty. Boldly walking in, she began to sing as sweetly as possible. The Rough People gathered around her.

She said boldly to the leader, "These beautiful sounds which you have just heard came from these things on my face and neck. I'm ready to let you have them if you will give me some of your precious stones. I don't wish to part with such a beautiful voice, but since I know you would very much like to have it, I am making you this offer!"

The leader advanced a few steps and said, "So you are making us a generous offer, are you? All right, close your eyes!"

Yu-Wen closed her eyes happily. Her plans were proceeding smoothly. "Open your eyes now," cried the leader.

Yu-Wen put her hands to her face. Imagine her horror when she found that instead of a smooth skin, she touched more warts than before! There were six more warts on her forehead where there had been four, three more on each cheek and twice the number on her chin and neck!

"What's the meaning of this?" shouted Yu-Wen.

"Ha, ha, ha!" laughed the Rough People. "Ha, ha, ha!"

The leader explained, "You intended to trick us, and cheat us of our precious stones! We found that even with those warts on our faces and necks we could make no beautiful sounds. So we took them off and kept them in a bag. We regretted giving the lady who came here before you the precious stones, but really, it wasn't her fault. Then you came along and tried to cheat us. Well, since you said you were unwilling to part with your beautiful voice, you can keep it, together with the beautiful voice of that first lady. That's why we've given you her warts as well! Ha, ha, ha!"

They then told her to leave their cave and never bother them again.

Yu-Wen stumbled home in the darkness. She covered her face and neck with a large piece of cloth, not daring to show herself to anybody. Her mother was horrified to find her covered with more warts than she had left the house with, but there was nothing she could do.

For the rest of her days, Yu-Wen stayed in the house with a piece of cloth covering her face and neck. As for Yin-Fei, her beauty soon attracted a rich and powerful prince who married her and brought her much happiness and prosperity.

THE FAITHFUL SERVANT

NO SERVANT HAD a better master than Yue Yang. This elderly gentleman was very rich and lived in a large mansion with his wife and children. He was a magistrate and had immense power, but never once did he abuse this power.

He was known far and wide for his sense of justice and his firmness in dealing with those who were dishonest or unfair in their treatment of their subordinates. Most of all, Yue Yang was known for his compassion and kindness to the poor and suffering. No beggar ever left his doors with his stomach still empty or body still naked. Yue Yang gave orders to his servants to be kind always to those who came begging at his door.

To his servants, Yue Yang was the perfect master. He was always considerate and kind in his treatment of them, never shouting at them or beating them. He was firm, but always fair with those servants who proved dishonest or deceitful. These, however, were few. In general, he was so much loved and respected by his servants that they were only too willing to serve him till the end of their lives.

Now, of these servants, there was one named Jiang Yi whom Yue Yang loved best of all. Jiang Yi had been in Yue Yang's service since he was a little boy. His father had served Yue Yang till the day of his death. Jiang Yi, now a strong, fine young man, was always ready to serve his master to the best of his capacity. There was nothing he would not do for Yue Yang whom he loved as a father.

Between master and servant then, there was a bond of strong love. The other servants were not in the least bit jealous of the favour shown to Jiang Yi, probably because Jiang Yi was always pleasant to them and never used his special position to bully them.

The years went by. Yue Yang was growing old, but he was still strong and alert. Jiang Yi continued to serve his master faithfully.

One day, Jiang Yi was struck by a mysterious illness. It left him pale, cold, delirious and on the point of death. Yue Yang was most alarmed. He was afraid this servant whom he loved as his own son would die.

He called in the best physicians but it was no use. No cure was in sight. Jiang Yi lay close to death's door.

One evening, in weariness and despair, Yue Yang took a walk. He walked on and on, not caring which path he took and only thinking how he could save Jiang Yi. "What a pity if such a fine, noble, loyal servant should die! He is not yet past youth!" thought Yue Yang sadly.

There was a slight drizzle and Yue Yang turned to retrace his steps to his mansion. In the darkness, however, he found that he had lost his way. He walked on and saw, in the light of a flash of lightning, that he was in a strange place — a place of waste ground with a few leafless trees. He was about to seek shelter from the rain when he heard a voice calling his name.

Turning round he saw a woman. She was an old woman, quite ugly to look at.

"Yue Yang," she said, "you are very sad because

your beloved servant Jiang Yi is dying. Indeed, he will die tonight."

"Oh, no, no!" cried Yue Yang. "I don't want him to die!"

"You have sought a cure for his illness all over the province but have failed," the old woman continued.

Yue Yang then realised that he was talking to no ordinary mortal. This old woman displaying so much knowledge and meeting him in this dark, strange place was a ghost!

"Yes, I am what you think," she said, reading his thoughts. She continued, "Yue Yang, I have a proposal to make. I will make your beloved servant Jiang Yi well. In return, you must agree to meet me

within seven days of his recovery!"

Yue Yang knew what she wanted. She would take him away with her to the ghost world that she had come from! In his studies he had read of ghosts and the demands they made in return for favours.

"No!" cried Yue Yang, but the picture of the dying Jiang Yi returned to his mind to torture him. He thought, "I am growing old — even my beard is beginning to show white hairs, whereas Jiang Yi is still young. Besides, with his noble qualities, he will do much good in this world."

Thinking of all this, he agreed to the ghost's proposal.

Yue Yang hurried home, and lo and behold! Who should come running to meet him but Jiang Yi himself! The young man had been restored to life! He greeted his master with great devotion and exclaimed on his good fortune in having the dreadful illness leave him so quickly and completely. "Now I shall be able to serve you better, my dear and kind master," said the loyal Jiang Yi.

Yue Yang was now in torment. In seven days, he would have to meet the ghost. In seven days, he himself would be dead, carried off to the world of ghosts! Yue Yang groaned secretly in his distress. He feared to die, but having made a promise, he would keep it.

Yue Yang did not breathe a word of his encounter to either his wife or to Jiang Yi. Yet they noticed that he was troubled. He could neither eat nor sleep.

Jiang Yi was most distressed to see his beloved master in such a state. He begged to know the cause, promising to do anything to relieve even a small part of the suffering. Yue Yang only shook his head.

"No," he said sorrowfully. "Nobody can help me. I must face everything alone."

On the fifth day after his recovery, Jiang Yi was in Yue Yang's room, seeing to the comfort of his beloved master who had grown thin and pale. Yue Yang was asleep. It was a fitful sleep broken by frightful dreams.

"Yes, if you will cure my belóved servant, I shall meet you here within seven days of his recovery," Yue Yang muttered in his sleep.

Jiang Yi drew closer to the bed. He listened very carefully as the old man continued to talk in his sleep. Now he understood the cause of Yue Yang's distress. He was struck by the love his master had shown for him.

"I won't let him go to that ghost! He must not die!" cried Jiang Yi grimly. He knew it would be useless to persuade him to forget his promise, for Yue Yang had never broken his word in his whole life. Jiang Yi thought hard of how he could save his master.

"He is such a kind, wise, noble man with much wealth and power whereas I am only a servant," thought Jiang Yi. "His death would be a greater loss than mine!"

Then Jiang Yi had an idea. He whispered to Yue Yang who was still tossing about restlessly and muttering to himself. "Which robe did you wear on the night you met the ghost? Which cap? Which slippers?"

Yue Yang answered freely, his eyes closed. "They are all hidden in the chest behind the bed. I did not wish to look anymore upon the clothes that had been in a ghost's presence!"

Jiang Yi took the robe, cap and slippers and left the room.

On the seventh night, Jiang Yi put these articles on secretly while everybody was asleep. He also attached a false beard that looked like Yue Yang's to his chin. Then he put on Yue Yang's spectacles.

Silently, he stole out of the house. He sped in the darkness to the strange place to meet the ghost . . .

"Where is Jiang Yi?" demanded Yue Yang the next morning. He was fully recovered.

None of the servants knew. One of them said he thought he saw Jiang Yi do something strange. He put on the master's clothes and then left the house in a hurry.

"My clothes?" said Yue Yang, puzzled.

Suddenly he recollected that somebody had asked him the night before last what he had worn on the night he met the ghost. It must have been Jiang Yi. Yue Yang then understood Jiang Yi's plans. He quickly called for a horse and rode to the spot where he had met the ugly woman, the ghost.

He found, on the ground, a heap of clothes and knew at once that he was too late. The faithful Jiang Yi, according to the plan he had formulated while listening to his master's muttering, had been mistaken for his master by the ghost. The ghost had carried him off, leaving the pile of clothes behind. Yue Yang wept over the loss of this faithful servant who had sacrificed his life for him.